The Riddlemaster

For Miriam and Danylo with love— K.C.H.

To E, A, C and Mo— S.J.

Published by Tradewind Books in Canada and the UK in 2016
Text copyright © 2015 Kevin Crossley-Holland
Illustrations copyright © 2016 Stéphane Jorisch

Book design by Elisa Gutiérrez
The text of this book is set in Grenale Slab. Title type is Mussica Antiqued.

10   9   8   7   6   5   4   3   2   1

. . . .

LIBRARY AND ARCHIVES CANADA CATALOGUING IN PUBLICATION

Crossley-Holland, Kevin, author
    The riddlemaster / Kevin Crossley-Holland ; illustrations
by Stéphane Jorisch.

ISBN 978-1-926890-11-1 (hardback)

    I. Jorisch, Stéphane, illustrator II. Title.

PZ7.C9394Ri 2016   j823'.914   C2015-902989-9

. . . .

Printed and bound in Canada on ancient forest-friendly paper.

The publisher thanks the Government of Canada and Canadian Heritage for their financial
support through the Canada Council for the Arts, the Canada Book Fund and Livres Canada
Books. The publisher also thanks the Government of the Province of British Columbia for the
financial support it has given through the Book Publishing Tax Credit program and the British
Columbia Arts Council.

Kevin Crossley-Holland

The Riddlemaster

illustrations by Stéphane Jorisch

Tradewind Books

VANCOUVER • LONDON

Anouk and Ben and Cara stood on the scribbly
tideline and watched waves breaking into blues.
"Blue of blue," said Anouk.
"Every blue there is," Ben said.

"Even the ones without names," added Anouk.
   Side by side they stood and stared across the bouncy
sea at the little island.

"It looks like a gold coin," said Anouk.
   "I bet there's treasure," Ben said, "if only we could get there."

"Maybe you can," croaked a voice.
    The old man's face was as wrinkled as monkey-puzzle bark. He was all bones and light as a tail-feather.

"But it's very, very risky," the old man said.

"Have you got a boat?" asked Ben.

"I ask the questions. I'm the Riddlemaster."

"Riddlemaster!" exclaimed Anouk. "I like riddles."

"The islanders will sail you across," the old man told them, "but you won't be able to go on shore unless you can answer seven riddles."

Cara blew out her cheeks like a teapot.

"What if we can't answer them?" Anouk asked.

The boat was jam-packed with islanders.

On one side were Wolf, and Wildcat with her litter of wild kittens, and three Bears, and Beast, and Dragon; on the other side were friendly Donkey, and Cockerel, and Dog, and leaping Hare, and gentle, shining Unicorn.

Crocodile swam along just behind the boat.

"Are you ready?" Riddlemaster demanded.

Anouk put her arms round Ben's and Cara's shoulders.

"This is the first riddle," Riddlemaster told them, "and it's quite easy: *What do you have to keep when you give it?*"

"I know that one," Anouk replied at once. "When you give your word, you have to keep it."

"You do," Riddlemaster agreed. "All aboard now!"

The boat's mast was a soaring word-tree. It had thousands and thousands of leaves and each fluttering leaf had one word painted on it.

Up top, a Carrion-Crow perched in the crow's nest.

Beast stood up on his hind legs. "I know a riddle," he growled.
"*What walks on four legs in the early morning, and two legs at lunchtime, and three legs in the evening?*"

Ben put up his right hand. "We did that at school. Four
legs . . . two legs . . . I can't remember."

Beast, and Wildcat, and Wolf, the three Bears, and Dragon
surrounded the three children. They licked their lips.

"Oh, yes," said Ben quickly. "Yes, I can. It's a person. A baby crawls on all fours. Children and grown-ups walk on two legs. And some old people need a cane."

Friendly Donkey brayed, and Cockerel crowed, and Dog barked, and leaping Hare whistled, and gentle Unicorn smiled.

"That's two right," the old man said. "But there are still five more."

"I've got a riddle," spat Wildcat. "If only . . . if only my . . . Sshh!
Ssshhh! For pity's sake, SSHH!"

   "Hurry up, Mrs Wildcat," Riddlemaster told her.

   "*Pity those who have them. Pity those who don't.*"

   "Don't what?" Ben asked.

   "Have them," Anouk said.

   "Dear ones!" wheedled Mrs Wildcat. "Darlings! Sshhh! For
pity's sake, SSSHHH!"

"Oh! I get it," said Anouk. "*Pity those who have them. Pity those who don't.* Children!"

Then Wildcat, and Wolf, and Beast, and the three Bears, and Dragon all shook their heads, and groaned, and moaned.

"Just in time," Riddlemaster growled.

"Woof!" barked Dog. "*What have heads like dogs, and feet like dogs, and tails like dogs, but aren't dogs?*"

"Cats," said Ben.

"No, they don't," Anouk said. "Cats don't have heads like dogs."

"Oh no!" said Ben.

Again Wolf, and Wildcat, and the three Bears, and Beast, and Dragon pressed round the three children. They licked their lips and bared their teeth.

Ben stared up at all the leaves springing and leaping and frolicking in the word-tree. "Is the answer . . . well, is it puppies?"

"All right!" snapped Crocodile from behind the boat. "This is the fifth riddle and it isn't easy. *My eyes are in the middle of my chest, and my flesh is inside my bones. What am I?*"

"Ugly," Ben replied.

"No," snapped Crocodile. He opened his jaws and lashed and splashed the water with his tail.

Then Ben saw how the old man's head was sunken, and he was all bones.

"I know," he said, grinning. "It's the Riddlemaster!"

Anouk clamped her hand over Ben's mouth.
"Well," she said, "shellfish have got flesh
inside their bones . . ."
"Crabs," exclaimed Ben. "Crabs or lobsters."
Crocodile clapped his jaws shut in surprise.
Carrion-Crow spread his black wings
and stared down from the crow's nest.
It cawed, "*What crosses in front of the
sun, without making any shadow?*"

"Each riddle's more difficult than the one before," complained Ben. "I don't know."

A strong, warm gust shook all the word-tree's shiny leaves and rocked the boat.

"Oh!" exclaimed Anouk. "What about . . ."

WHOOSH!

"What?" croaked Riddlemaster. "What did you say?"

WHOOSH!

"I can't hear you," Riddlemaster said, "and if I can't hear you, you haven't guessed the riddle."

Wildcat, and Wolf, and the three Bears, and Beast, and Dragon all crowded round the three children. They licked their lips and bared their teeth.

"Wind!" cried Anouk. "WIND! Wind crosses in front of the sun without making a shadow."

"Look at the island," said Ben. "It's waiting for us."

"Now for the seventh riddle," growled Riddlemaster in a dark voice.

"What if we can't answer it?" Anouk and Ben asked.

"*What's the treasure you can keep and share at the same time?*" the old man asked.

"Not a secret?" asked Ben.

"No," said Anouk very quickly. "No, Ben, it's not."

"Not a secret," said Ben.

"Your time's running out," Riddlemaster croaked.

"The treasure you can keep . . ." said Anouk.

"I'm warning you," Riddlemaster growled.

Then Wildcat, and Wolf, and Beast, and the three Bears, and Dragon all reached out for the three children again, and they all began to sing a terrible, hungry song.

"Wait!" cried Cara.

But the islanders screeched, and howled, and snarled, and roared, and growled.

"Can you hear how impatient they are?" asked Riddlemaster. "For the last time—*What's the treasure you can keep and share?*"

Cara took hold of Anouk's left hand and Ben's right hand. She stared up at the singing word-tree.

Then she turned to the old man. "Is it a story?" she asked in a small voice.

"Yes!" cried Riddlemaster. "A story! So now you're ready to meet the islanders, and they're all waiting to share their stories with you."

Anansi and Anne of Green Gables, Ali Baba and Arthur, Ayakashi and Beauty and the Beast, Peter Rabbit and Baba Yaga, the Cat in the Hat, Cinderella and Coyote, Elk Hunter, Frog Prince, Firebird and Fu Xi, Goldilocks, Huckleberry Finn and John Henry ... a whole alphabet of islanders greeted Anouk, Ben and Cara.

"And when you get home," Riddlemaster promised them, "you can share your own story, too."